Rosa Sardà   Rosa M. Curto

I Like Hiding
Me gusta esconderme

English text by Bernice Randall

LECTORUM
PUBLICATIONS, INC.

"They won't see us under the bed!"

−¡No nos verán debajo de la cama!

"Where are you?" Mommy asks.

–¿Dónde están? –pregunta mami.

"Who is it?"

"Those are Grandma's feet."

–¿Quién es?

–Son los pies de abuela.

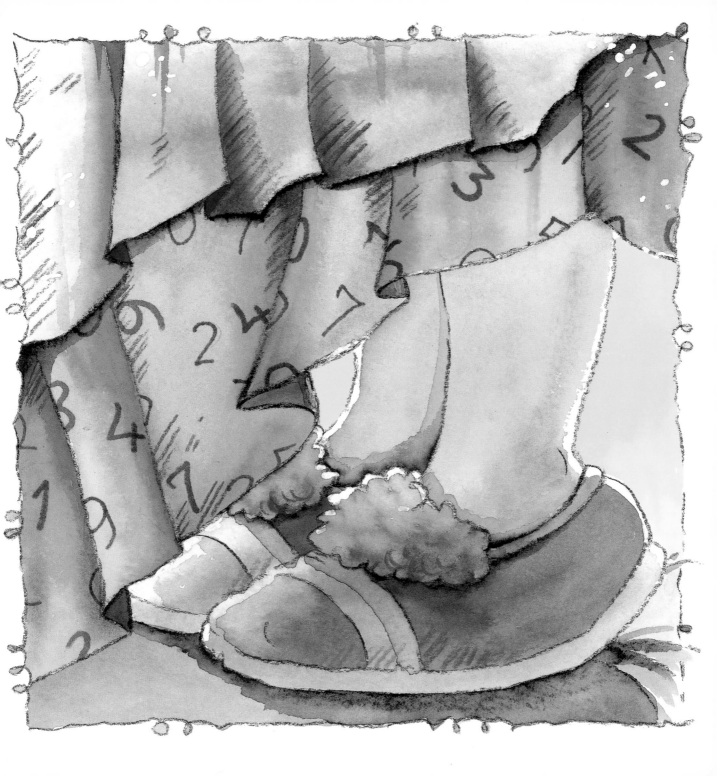

"Look! Daddy's shoes!"

—¡Mira, los zapatos de papi!

"One paw, two paws, three paws, four paws... It's the cat!"

–Una pata, dos patas, tres patas, cuatro patas... ¡Es el gato!

"Kids, where are you?"
Mommy asks.

–Niños, ¿dónde están?
–pregunta mami.

"They can't find us!"

–¡No nos encuentran!

"One foot, two feet, three feet, four feet... Who is it?"

–Un pie, dos pies, tres pies, cuatro pies... ¿Quién es?

16

"I don't know who it is!"

"Neither do I!"

–¡No sé quién es!

–¡Yo tampoco!

"This is s-c-a-r-y!"

–¡Qué miedooo!

"I found you! Don't be afraid.
It's me," says Mommy.

–¡Los encontré! No se asusten,
soy yo –dice mami.

I LIKE HIDING
ME GUSTA ESCONDERME

Bilingual Edition

This edition published by arrangement with the original publisher
Combel Editorial, S. A., for the United States and Puerto Rico

ISBN 1-930332-30-0
D.L. M-13987-2002
Printed in Spain

10 9 8 7 6 5 4 3 2 1